Y0-CKN-770

Praise for
Deer Michigan

Jack Buck's prose is sharp and surgical, perfect for probing everything from the coming water wars to the interior lives of birds. Buck's interests and insights range far and wide. So do his affections: in gentler stories he offers homages to Jack Kerouac and Jim Harrison, an ode to late-night winter road trips, some tough love for Detroit—all of it delivered in a highly personal, arrestingly intimate voice.

Lean as they are, Jack Buck's stories also deliver some stunning atmospherics: "What else was there to do in early March with the Michigan wind blowing snow into everyone's house?" There are moments of willful exile; spontaneous escape; even a bizarre encounter with Mao, a devoted practitioner, in his dotage, of small naps (who knew?). Each of these brief stories is a window on a world of Buck's choosing; it's our good fortune that he inhabits so many worlds at once, and such fascinating ones. In their very compression the stories invite us to focus on the people and things nearest to us while never losing sight—not once—of what beckons from the far horizon.

~ Edward Hamlin, author of *Night in Erg Chebbi and Other Stories*

Jack Buck's collection is more than a play on words for the title, it's word play, story after story. *Dead Jack Kerouac* is a one long sentence story with a forgetful narrator trying his hardest to tell a Kerouac anecdote that begins with, "Forget how it goes." A brilliant concept and an equally brilliant opening. Another favorite of mine could only have been written by a baseball fan, *Detroit Hustles Harder.* Again, Buck comes up with a great premise and has the chops to pull it off. His *Great Flood* story opens with prostitutes and drug dealers escaping a flood by seeking shelter in a bookstore. That's enough of a tease to make you want to read this story and the entire collection. Buck has a unique voice and writing style and this is a book you'll not only want to read but one you'll want to share.

~ Paul Beckman, author of *Peek: a flash collection*

"Something quite wonderful happens when you allow yourself to drift through life without a plan of direction," writes Jack Buck in his poignant debut story collection. The writing in *Deer Michigan* takes this philosophy to heart, embracing the flux of fate in over fifty ethereal narratives. In one story we meet an exiled Mao on a hiking trail, in another the narrator mourns the graceful disappearance of birds. Buck's stories ripple with nostalgia, a reverence for the natural world and an America with room in which to wander. Though the stories in *Deer Michigan* are short—in one case spun out in a single sentence—they bottle up an expanse of human experience, offering us a stunning universe of feeling.

~ Allegra Hyde, author of *Of This New World*

Jack Buck's writing here is not trying to trick or dazzle you. It moves with a sincerity that invokes the past and future into a tender present. And from this tender present, *Deer Michigan* allows us to re-imagine possibilities of being and feeling.

~ Steven Dunn, author of *Potted Meat*

Loose and freewheeling, yet compact, these stories by Jack Buck are streamed through with insight and emotion. The stories of *Deer Michigan* are quietly startling, awake, and original. Highly recommended.

~ Kathy Fish, author of *Wild Life*, *Rift* and *Together We Can Bury It*

Jack Buck's surreal, stream-of-consciousness pieces are populated with dictators, ghosts, and regular folks. His characters confront water shortage, root for the Detroit Tigers, and talk to migrating birds. Prepare yourself for the environmental apocalypse by reading this book!

~ Kathleen Founds, author of *When Mystical Creatures Attack!*

Deer Michigan

stories by

Jack C. Buck

TRUTH SERUM PRESS

TRUTH SERUM PRESS

All stories in this collection copyright © Jack C. Buck
First published as a collection December 2016

All rights reserved by the author and publisher. Except for brief excerpts used for review or scholarly purposes, no part of this book may be reproduced in any manner whatsoever without express written consent of the publisher or the author.
Any historical inaccuracies are made in error.

This book is a work of fiction and there is no intended resemblance to persons living, who have lived, or who will live.

ISBN: 978-1-925536-25-6

Truth Serum Press
4 Warburton Street
Magill SA 5072
Australia

Email: truthserumpress@live.com.au
Website: http://truthserumpress.net
Truth Serum Press catalogue: http://truthserumpress.net/catalogue/

Front cover design by Jack. C. Buck
Front cover photographs:
top & middle © Jack C. Buck / bottom © Republica @ Pixaby

Author photograph by Dylan Osborne

Also available as an eBook
ISBN: 978-1-925536-26-3

"Someday Time will die, and Love will bury it."

~ Richard Brautigan

For my family and friends

Contents

National Forest Health Monitoring Program

The church is located east of town, before the open pastoral, where the river opens up. It's a church in the sense of a gathering place, not of being a structure like a traditional church. They all slept at the church, on the ground, against a tree, watching the light from the sun pass through the dense forest of the church's non-wall bedroom.

I would sit, back against a tree, watching; and whoever felt like it would go down and stand in the middle of the church's aisle, waist deep in church river, raising their hands towards the sky as if to touch it, half expecting God to lift and carry them up like that. That would be nice I thought, if God really did take them with. Happy and sad, we would see each other again.

For Matthew

Today I am thinking of you and Michigan. I remember all the books we collected, stacked on the floor against the wall, and the alley-found mattress angled between the kitchen and bathroom. *One weighs one's purchases of necessity* is something you would have said. Somewhere in there when the money ran out, we stopped going to the bar, instead we pooled the occasional dollar to buy a cheap bottle. I don't think it was ever much about the whiskey, it was more about the walks to the store.

A radio, either turned up or turned low, played forever that summer. I remember it raining a lot. It always rained when we wanted it to, when we felt like talking and staying in all night. On nights like those, we stayed up late, our shadows twelve feet tall against the wall, laughing, planning what we were going to do with our lives. Then, at some point, late in the night, our insides would only talk, silent on the outside, pretending not to know this wouldn't be forever, already missing one another.

It's As If We Never Left

There you are and there I am and over there is everyone else you know or have met one time or another. And over there is the center of the town, the library, the bar, the defunct theater the town hasn't replaced because of lack of money. What about the road, the alley, the porch, the side door, the pile of coats, the broken stairs leading to the cold basement where some of our friends decided to make their bedroom. Up the stairs is the oversized kitchen, the deep sink that made everyone excitable about all the big dinners we would have together. It's like those 1892 original homeowners knew we were coming to live here. Let's walk backwards down those roads, let's sleep in the front lawns of the old houses you liked in particular – they won't see us, they won't mind. Look, there's the table, and the wood flooring that reminded you of your grandparent's house. Here is the bowl you put fruit in; here is the bucket of paint to paint the wall like you always wanted to. How come? Why didn't you paint that wall? I bet that wall would have looked real good painted. You should come back, I'll drive out and be there in three days to pick you up. This time I won't not say anything, this time I'll say let's get up, let's get after it, it's something we can make together. We can paint those walls together, a color we both like, and it will be like we never left.

Somewhere in the Future You Are Remembering Today

You found out rather painfully that love moves to places like New York without giving two weeks notice. You want to see something else happen, but it just doesn't. But, you and she had a good time with it all. You try to rationalize it; making lists keeps you somewhat sane. It's the start of something else, as someone one day before now said to someone else in a similar situation. She said New York City is the greatest place in the whole world, and she had to go back. You remember her saying it had something to do with the timing just not being quite right. Perhaps if you had met a month or two before, but she had already made up her mind to move back east. What could you say? No, don't leave; stay with me? A few months would pass, and she would eventually grow tired of the couples-sex.

That's the way it goes is a cheap, overused position of mind to take, so you'll try to find a better job here soon to justify why you stayed and didn't go. You'll write a list, rigging it where the cons outweigh the pros of whether or not to move to New York with her. You'll type up twenty-seven-and-a-half copies to keep in various drawers around the house, in case over time the one taped to the fridge needs a new replacement.

Filling in

I would walk next to her, a foot or two behind her, trying to keep up. She would lean into it, talking, singing a few lines in between from a song that reminded her of what she was talking about. In those rare moments when she wasn't moving, at crosswalks, sometimes I would say something when I felt it was worth something, and she would look at me, smiling, ready to grab my arm to encourage me to go on.

And then she would really keep at it. I close my eyes to slow it down. I want her to slow down, but this is her speed. I want her to look at me, instead of telling me I can have her anyway I want. She likes everything, she says. She tells me to tell her what I want. I want to tell her to breathe hard and wait for it. I want to kiss her inner thighs, her eyelids, but I don't want to disturb her. This is how she does life, I'm just here. So, this will have to do. I don't want to see her frown and upset as though she has remembered who I am, and who I am not.

Back to the Beginning

By not talking about it, we both believed it gave an exciting feeling to our friendship and of what could have been. I never intended to act on my feelings, yet I knew if there was ever a moment to tell her, it had to be now.

Looking, but not really looking, we sat on the bench. Probably a 7-year-old ran by in circles with a mother telling her daughter to keep near. The wind blew. Time didn't know what to do.

"Nature does nothing uselessly." Aristotle said that, she said, glancing over at me, smiling.

"Is that right," I replied.

She thought I would go on to say more, but I didn't.

I came close, once, to really saying it.

We met back in undergraduate. We kept in touch over the last 8 years. When I would visit Michigan for a week or two in the summer months, we always made a point to have dinner together, walk around the lake to talk and laugh.

I wanted to go back to the beginning, when and where we first met. I want to wander the old Michigan roads that lead into the woods. I want to stand on the bridge that overlooks the river, where I jumped off in hopes of trying to scare you; where we both sat under the bridge in the late afternoon to watch the train overhead roll off further north. I wanted to tell you then.

Cities in the Wilderness

I watched my first snowflake of the year on the corner of 13th and Broadway while waiting at a red light. A second or two faster and I would have missed it, turning left, going through the changing yellow light, onto moving southbound traffic, where I wouldn't have noticed, mistaking the snowflake as just a November pre-snow-rain-bead.

That snowflake got me thinking, about last July when Francis was in bed on a Sunday at 2 in the afternoon, and I was out back in the then prospering garden of zucchini and cucumber. I read a poem out there in that garden written by Richard Brautigan; he described a 1965, San Francisco snowstorm he witnessed in his backyard, in his garden: He uncoiling the hose to put away till next spring, staring up, while a single snowflake fell, then suspended itself midair for his eyes to take notice of time and season floating on.

A Brief History of the Great Lakes Region in the 1990s

Dad went to work; he sold life insurance policies to farmers. Mom woke up with us at 5:30 to make breakfast. By that time, two years in, the paper route had lost its excitement; however, Dad would plead for us at the dinner table to keep with it.

We had to wear uniforms at school, blue pants, tucked in oxford shirts. You could wear turtlenecks, but rarely anyone ever did. During college football season, on Fridays at school, we were allowed to wear our Notre Dame sweatshirts. There were no other colleges. Dad would convince me to not quit the paper route by saying, "Don't you want to save up your money so you can go to school in South Bend?"

It was expected for us to deliver the 5 blocks of newspapers by 7:30, otherwise old men who read the paper would make a point to be waiting for us out front with a cast-iron snow shovel. Mom believed in the respect of punctuality, so in those last few months of the paper route she would drive us around in the 1992 Chrysler Town and Country Van. Mom behind the wheel robed in Dad's long, gray winter jacket with the red plaid inner-lining, while I ran through the neighborhood to and from the van winging rolled up newspapers onto porches. We really made good time when Mom finally bought in. The system involved having the side door swung open while she drove at a consistent slow speed of 5mph. It saved me time on opening and closing the heavy door. We really had a good thing going.

Then, over dinner one evening, Mom told us we were going to have an addition to the family. The paper route was now going to be solely up to me. Mom wouldn't be driving me around with George coming soon. I had grown to like the van-delivery system. I was able to warm up in the car a bit in between blocks.

It was right before our school's winter break when I quit delivering the newspaper. At first I would just not deliver to a block or two, telling anyone if they complained perhaps a stranger is ripping off the neighborhood's papers. Blaming the lost papers on the evening's snowfall bought me time as well. Eventually in the last weeks of the job I managed to find enough sewer gutters to shove the papers down.

It was the coldest winter in a decade, Notre Dame had lost in the Fiesta bowl to Ohio State, and Jenny O'Brien had switched schools. I saw no point. Jenny was what made sense for Catholic schools to be all boys or girls. We had no business being around 300 girls in hiked up socks wearing wool skirts. I don't think us boys who were lucky enough to have our assigned seats within a seat or two remembered a single concept taught that semester.

There was something about the class location being across the courtyard, the half-lit basement storage room turned carpeted classroom that added to the excitement of it all. None of us were ever late or absent for that class. When she was, we all died a little inside, contemplating the worst had happened. Perhaps Jenny switched schools. It was all her father's fault, he probably took a management job, the family now had to move up to Milwaukee. Us boys wanted to hunt down Jenny's father. We wanted to tell him a thing or two.

write talk-talk if you have no one to talk-talk with

1. Wear a raincoat even if you have no idea whether it is supposed to rain or not.

2. Cover the apartment floor vents if you are open to the idea of the neighbor living downstairs listening in with the CIA.

3. Tape collage art over the TV screen until you finally remember the name of that one movie you have wanted to watch.

4. Read poems and short stories written by people who don't have a book deal.

5. Walk down streets in your city you have never walked down even though it takes longer to get where you are going.

6. When you want certain moments to last longer say the word Mississippi before and after each second said aloud.

7. When you want to write but it just seems like something you can't quite figure out is making it hard to do, replace standard sized paper with 5 by 7 inch paper so the pages fill up easier.

8. If you're not one to save stuff, use movie and concert ticket stubs as bookmarks or as kindling for a fire.

9. Learn to cook something new this week.

10. Tell your friends and family what you had for dinner last night.

11. Bond with coworkers you normally don't talk with over the memory and promise of good food by way of food talk, maybe it will lead to other promising conversation, like, what good HBO shows you are both currently watching when you get home from work.

12. Buy a second hand shirt at a thrift store that doesn't fit you but will look good on a friend, tell them you saw it and thought of them.

13. Go move away if you want to then move back if you want to, but make sure to tell people an elaborate uncontrollable reason of why you moved back because people like to hear good stories that they can tell other people.

14. Ride the city bus all day and listen for signs of which numbers to pick for the next lotto drawing.

15. Fill in your wall calendar with birthday reminders of your favorite dead people.

16. Make sure to go to bed early once in a while to give your body rest.

17. Notice the effects of what foods you are eating in correlation with your daily energy levels.

18. Don't use the word "all" when arguing an issue.

19. Openly talk about sex with your partner to help with each other's self esteem.

20. Buy stamps and consider mailing the occasional letter.

21. Keep a chest or box in your childhood basement to fill with stuff to keep forever, even if it's painfully embarrassing.

22. Be thankful if you had a childhood home and liked living there.

23. Know when someone isn't doing you any good and plan accordingly to find someone better for you.

24. Be alone for stretches in your life.

25. Ask for help from friends when your mind is saying negative things to you.

26. Smile and acknowledge people who otherwise walk with their head down living unnoticed.

27. When you find yourself living in a big city don't let it be an excuse to not introduce yourself to the neighbor across the street.

28. Keep conversations going either in talk-talk or write-talk sort of like this.

29. Keep going.

home

Somewhere there's a violin and a guitar and a song and a room and people are in this room, and some are sitting on the ground, and someone is hiding under a table after having just heard a poem read about them, and others are standing in the kitchen next to the window that's stuck and won't close using the stove as a light, and two or three are singing all different songs but the same song at once, and there is a friend bringing over knockoff speed later who hasn't arrived yet and he is bringing three or eight other people with him whom you haven't met yet and probably two of these people will end up staying for two and half weeks and one will never leave and one will end up moving out to Denver with you, and over the years more of them will decide to make Denver their new home because why not? And also because everyone needs a place to call home and it doesn't matter where that place is as long as you are with others who like having you around, and it's the best when you really like them too, and when you meet people like this they stay with you and you think of them a lot and you miss them and you love them and write about them, and when you meet people of this sort a nice thing happens where Wichita, Denver, a parking lot, Oregon, the woods of northern Michigan, and the backseat of a car on the way to San Antonio all become home if you want it to. And, so, I will go anywhere as long as you are there and I am with you, and wherever that may be we can call that place home too.

Grow Old Like Herman

The Dow Jones finished up 153.49 at 16461, ending a three-day slump. All the while, Herman ran his daily errands, as an old man, if he is lucky enough does, because, no offense, but, Herman doesn't care about the Dow Jones. He has better things to think about.

As the world is, people have stopped noticing Herman, and that's sad. If anyone ever did, we wouldn't know of it, and that's sad, too. But, Herman understands, and forgives the people of America because he knows they don't know any better.

These mornings Herman bothers with very little besides doing what he wants in his means. If you are lucky you too will grow old and live a life like Herman. And, like Herman, you will come to age and possess what Herman holds, that measurable and stackable substance that comes with time.

Deer Michigan

Dear lakes and woods and forests. Dear 10:14 June 21st sunset. Dear deers. Dear deers that have escaped collision and death and lived to tell about it to their brothers and sisters. Dear early fall and long winter. Dear day trips to Chicago and back home by midnight. Dear Saturday afternoon college football when the whole town shuts down to come together to watch the game. Dear lots of rain. Dear people who were laid-off from the factory. Dear wool tube socks that we all got for Christmas. Dear old Tigers Stadium. Dear farms. Dear weathered barn on a no longer existing farm. Dear cider mill. Dear Faygo pop. Dear small towns where you can get by on not much. Dear missing school because of five feet of snow. Dear neighborhood we grew up in that made us feel like we were all in this thing together. Dear families with seven kids and three bedrooms to a family. Dear Mom and Dad. Dear Michigan and your need for backup-always-ready-when-need-be coats. Dear those winter, rain, and spring coats that I just talked about. Dear Mom having me wear six layers under the red coat with the annoying zipper. Dear little brother Patrick years later wearing that same coat. Dear Dad and your unwillingness to sell off the old van. Dear old cold van with the broken heater I hope you are faring well wherever you are. Dear van is there a heaven? Dear van, are you in heaven, what's it like? Dear neighbor across the street who didn't believe in raking leaves, your protest always made sense to me. Dear rivers. Dear trees for letting us climb. Dear close streets and open spaces and all the neighbors and all the cities and all the people along the way.

a list of things to do, think, write, remember, look forward to, and consider

Things to do:
Fill out reimbursement form for work.
Buy that one book I've been meaning to buy.
Sell bicycle she left behind.
Get cash back from 7-Eleven in order to do the laundry across the street.
Get around to watching those movies my friends suggested.
Read an account of the beginning days of New Orleans, slaves and female French prisoners accompanied by nuns sent to Louisiana, only to be met by knowing Indians in the swamps who weren't buying what whitey was selling.

Things to think about:
How do I still remember when two years ago in passing, after ordering a burger late at night, walking home down Colfax, that one thing that one guy said, even now. We all have things, useful

things, useless things, things said, things done, that we remember for reasons we don't know, but want to know.

Things to write about:
The first televised baseball game 1939; Brooklyn Dodgers play the Cincinnati Reds, when only 400 people in New York City had televisions.

Things to remember:
My father moving around the house closing a squeaky window, summer rain.
Fall, I liked the smell of the neighborhood burning the leaves out in the street.
That Saturday morning, last summer, when I walked aimlessly seven miles to see what I was searching for – in a back alley, the young boy helping his father paint a garage.
The lentil soup doomsayers of rural Illinois.
The last catch and throw with my Dad before I thought I was too old for it.
Freshman year of high school, when you attended that party you had no business being at; you kissed the girl you had a crush on since 4th grade. You were both 14. She was embarrassed to like you. She told you never to tell anyone. I heard she married 2 or 3 years ago, moved to Ohio.

Things to look forward to:
Leftovers. Thanksgiving in a bag.
Next comes winter, then there's spring where people like to fall in love in the rain. Sounds nice.

Things to consider:
Perhaps God invented baseball, a game for those who can't find their lover. And maybe that's why God invented poetry for those times when there are no more games, when the season is over. For those stay up all night and write nights, where there's rerun programming on the radio in place of where the game ought to be.

Grand Rapids, Michigan

It was June and we were on fire. In certain areas of Michigan it wouldn't turn dark until after ten o'clock. We lived for the longest day of the year. We prepared for the date every summer. I remember the neighborhood friends cheering on the last of the evening light out there in the middle of the street, all because it was twelve minutes after ten and the street lights had yet to turn on. It was triumphant.

It was our street and everyone in the surrounding neighborhood knew so. Yet, every year during the first couple weeks of June we would have two or three people who would seem to forget this. Their miscalculation was in their failing to drive their car on through to the next block, avoiding our block altogether, past Alger to the south side of Raymond. And, when failing to do so, we would let them know by refusing to move out of the street, spitting on the cement, and hurling tennis balls at their car's headlights. They would all catch on after that.

I'm not sure what they were thinking. Perhaps they were hoping our families finally had enough and that we wouldn't be there this summer. Maybe they thought the lack of any air conditioning was just too much after 15 years and we collectively came to the agreement to finally take out a loan in order to all move to the better part of town, where all the homes come with a built in air conditioner. We weren't going anywhere though. We took pride in sweating it out. We felt tougher than the kids on the other side of town, and we made a point to beat their ass in whatever citywide recreational sport was in season at the time. We had to beat them. We wanted to make sure the rest of the world hadn't forgot about us.

And you know what else? We liked hearing our dads curse the heat and its humidity, it gave us an excuse to stay out late by not being in the house. "Get out there. Go to the lake. You're sleeping over at Oscar's house because his mom lets him have three box fans going all at once in the basement? Sure, don't blame ya, have a ball. Hm. Their electricity bill has gotta be through the roof. Do you know?" June 21st was always our favorite day of the year.

Mount Pleasant, Michigan

Frank had made the dive off the same tree into the same river every summer since the first time eleven years back when he was 12 years old. As then, when we were just young boys, and just as now, Thomas watched Frank make his way up the tree and bring himself out to the branch's end. When there were girls with the boys Frank would perform by scaling up the old, large tree rooted on the embankment of the river with double-speed. In what seemed like careless route he would fling himself out as far as his body would go, wrapping one precarious leg around the horizontal branch with his other leg dangling 100 feet high and 30 feet out above the surface of the water.

Frank was recognized as the best swimmer and most courageous of his friends. However, he was inflexible in being talked out of a potentially bad decision if he had already made up his mind. Everyone in town who knew Frank or of him all knew this. On the riverbank Thomas and the two girls, whom they had met earlier that afternoon, waited for Frank to show how it was to be properly done. Frank would say they all do it wrong. Frank believed there was a certain way one is to air oneself into a river. His way would vary slightly with each climb and plunge, but they all had a Frank quality to them.

The girls were putting their feet into the water. One of them talked for the other girl. The other girl Thomas thought was cute. Thomas had asked the other girl questions in hopes of beginning a further exchange, but she just quietly laughed and the other friend answered for her. Sometime a little after three in the afternoon Thomas had given up and only shrugged at the two girls. By this time Thomas had stopped noticing the girls and was looking out on the river. Every year, around this time, at the end of summer, Thomas would make a point to remember. Closing his eyes, with the warmth and pulsing geometric figures given by the late August sun his inner eye's darkness would explode with movement, reels, and stills of nature's offering before him.

It is then when Frank is letting go, knifing towards the river. Submerged, with the inside of the river around him, the ceiling of the river is shone with light, at the bottom, black.

A Reference to Weather

The other day at a bus stop where no bus was to come, I read an article about China's anti-rain campaign for the 2008 Olympics. China had plans to utilize airplanes, rocket launchers, and over 5,000 anti-aircraft guns in an attempt to stop rain from falling out of the sky. I've always talked about the weather; I picked up the habit from my father. When I was just a kid, in the summer after all day in the sun, I would sit out back in the screened-in porch to watch the rain. The cool of the wind and rain gave relief to my sun burnt shoulders. I liked when it rained then.

The rain is different now though. It's not a feel-good, about time, we needed some rain with all this dry weather. It's not even a heavy rain indicating summer is now over. It's a horizontal rain, don't bother with the umbrella, that soaks your shoes with a wind that rattles the hinges on the window. It's everyone else is weather-informed-prepared-citizens, and you don't know the day, month, or season. I used to be able to duck and contort my body through narrowing split second gaps that only a half-person could fit through, breaking myself free of the north avenue procession. For what has been maybe 6 months or 5 years I have been standing in a line, consisting of myself – at a stop, pickup, drop off, a leaving and going home.

Maybe I could do that other thing sometime. I want to do the other thing that the happy people do. Yeah, what they do, what you do. I've asked, but it won't work if they tell or show me how to do it. That's the difficulty in all of this. In fleeting pauses of realization, wait a minute here, I know what's going on, I stop strangers in the street to ask the time and what's the weekend weather. I hear all different answers.

I am waiting out in the rain, standing in stalled morning and evening traffic with a nonexistent raincoat and umbrella, in a six month to five-year storm. At a bus stop, with no bus coming to take me away from here.

Conversations in an Idle Car

You felt it earlier in the night, at dinner, in the way you responded by not responding to something she had said. You are relieved driving away back to your apartment that it didn't continue because for those other ones it isn't over when it ends, it goes on for some time afterward. Her voice, her smell, her hair sticks around. You find traces of her around, you turn up things you have nearly forgotten and it comes back to you.

You feel it, this shift, the turn, the this isn't going to work nice to have met you the last 4 or 5 weeks have been fine, but now it's over. It happens when it does and you see it when it does. And, her body, her legs, her arms look different now. I bet you probably slept over at her place on Monday.

Here it is Wednesday and you are talking and you notice from the corner of your eye her take a quick look at you to see if you are looking at her. She doesn't see that you see, so she shifts her body as far away from you in the passenger seat without unlocking the car's door and taking the gamble of tuck and roll at 45 miles per hour. She wants nothing to do with you anymore and tells you by looking out the window and saying, "Hm? What did you say?"

New Old Story

In the kitchen he poured another drink, looking at the bedroom that had only a mattress. The bed was stripped and the sheets were bunched beside on the ground. Supposedly the tiles were originally white. He tried warm water and white vinegar, but it had been too long since anyone had tried. As he sipped from the mug, he considered the pattern of the sheets: Her side, His side.

The reading lamp is now on top of the refrigerator. The nightstand she took, except for that, things looked much the way they had in the bedroom. He had emptied the drawers, stacked his pants and underwear in the closet, and sold the dresser last week. They had furnished the apartment when they moved to Denver and somehow got the apartment despite the twelve other hopeful renters waiting outside for the landlord to show up.

Let the young, ambitious couple at least have this for a while. The landlord had done her part; it was now up to this couple of what they would make of it. They moved in without inspecting anything; they told in a manner of asking that they would sign the lease right then and there. Everything save from the bed was purchased from an antique store in the neighborhood that was going out of business after 30 years.

Before the furniture, the couple's first purchase was the bed. It was "their" bed. And, before the bed, they held each other in one another's arms, and fell asleep on the floor like that, using three blankets as floor patting. Their bodies were sore and five short hours of sleep was normal, yet they didn't think to ever complain.

It wasn't until eight months after happily angling the large mattress up the stairs of their apartment did they begin complaining about the bed size being too small for the two of them.

When the Cubs Win the World Series

1. The Cubs win the World Series and Harry Caray is back from the dead. Someone is heard expressing his or her admiration for Harry's decision to be flown across the country from California in order to be buried in Chicago. We appreciate your family's decision, Harry, so thank you.

2. The city of Chicago burns down, but a planned fire this time around, not like that other one. And, you know what, it's a damn good fire, that only burns down stuff that benefits the good people of the city.

3. No one pays for anything during the three-week party, but somehow the good shop and restaurant owners don't lose out any in the city's free-for-all. Only bad business loses out, and they lose out big. People celebrate that, too.

4. The city places kitchenette tables on street corners so people can sit and talk with strangers about what the hell just happened.

5. People get to eat at restaurants they normally could never afford otherwise. But, with the choice, they still choose pizza because people like pizza, so people eat a lot of deep-dish pizza and freely take naps in the street.

6. There are expected delays on the 'L' train, but no one notices nor bothers to complain. It's a warmer than usual

November when this all happens, so the people wear their light jackets for comfort.

7. People are getting baptized in the fountain over at Grant Park.

8. A mile north on Michigan Ave, Billy Goat Tavern, the supposed cause of the 1945 World Series curse, is decidedly and fittingly the city's burning effigy. All the while, there is a pagan themed resurrection of some sort happening out in front of Wrigley Field in belief of summoning the ghosts of past Cubs. They deserve to party with us, the gathering crowd explains.

9. Politicians are being apprehended on their way out of the stadium by fans that work for the local unions. It's decided someone needs to be in charge, so people suggest the activists who were charged for protesting during the 1968 Democratic National Convention will do just fine. The activists are sworn in immediately and establish a committee to decide what's what. Also, The Chicago Housing Authority, CHA, is put on trial by mothers living in the south side projects. There is a rearrangement of leadership in the city. The natural order of just yesterday is no more.

10. By some freak phenomenon Lake Michigan is warm enough to swim in. White Sox fans and Cubs fans bathe together.

11. Random people say fuck it and get married on the spot. While this is happening, people who ought to get divorced will get divorced and they don't involve the lawyers. Because the lawyers are drunk and nobody's bothering to pick up their phone or go into work.

12. Doomsayers give up on religious fears and start getting really into baseball.

13. Cemeteries are visited by loved ones to tell their dead lovers and best friends that it happened. It finally really happened.

49 letters never mailed, to live out their days in a nonexistent shoe-box in a make believe attic

"What are you going to do with all of those letters?"

"Don't know."

"Well, I'm sure the people you wrote them to would like to receive some mail. No one writes letters anymore. Nowadays you can write anything in a letter and people will still be excited about it, probably put it up on their fridge all proud like."

Looking down at the kitchen tile, "Ha. I suppose you're right."

"What do you say in them anyways?"

"Not really sure. Stuff." Continuing, I consider, "Hm. Makes 'em kind of special and all, not mailing them, you know? With no one reading them. Hell, I don't even remember what they say, really."

"Yeah?" Shifting his weight from one leg to the other. "Interesting."

"Think about it. With the way things are now with technology and whatnot, there's no sense of unknown with us anymore. Everyone has said or will say, sooner rather than later, what they are going to say. I mean, even take us for example, here we are two friends who have known one another for some 10 years, yet in order to not bring upon a lapse we subconsciously feel the need to fill each moment with explanation and conversation. Why is that?"

Laughing now, "No shit."

"It's the reason why conversation is dead. I'm telling you man, like I've said, you gotta keep them guessing. These days, everyone knows everything, sometimes about things regarding yourself before you even know your own damn self."

"I hear ya."

"There's no magic anymore."

Sitting back down now, "Is that why you write?"

"Perhaps. Mostly just for fun. Never meant to take it too serious. But, hell, it's the only magic I know."

Almost There

A walking out of the woods, a clearing, after having been lost in dense pine for which seems like three or four long hours, or maybe it has been three or four years in a trackless forest. I can see myself when it happens, after all the turnarounds and switchbacks. The sun burns through the dawn fog. I am almost there.

How Hank Does It

I'm not going to tell you how to do it. I know as much as you. Though, making a list can help. I make lists. The lists are all rather comparable, for the most part. Admittedly, I'm too predictable as it is. It's in my best interest to look after what I add or claim to these lists. Comes with age, loss of love, the customary highs and lows of life, and making sure you don't find yourself doing things you don't want to be doing. Like, making Friday night plans three weeks in advance when you have no idea how you will be feeling on a particular evening at 7 o'clock, 21 days from now. I used to go along with plans like that, not anymore. What else, watching other people to see how they do it can help as well, if you come across the right person that is.

When making a list, consider things like the shockingly large amount of time spent just repeating indistinguishable conversations from one person to the next when your neighbor counts on you to consistently agree to a conversation each time you physically see one another. I once half-calculated the time, even wrote it down somewhere. It's why I now wait till nine at night to go down to do my laundry, and why I park my car three blocks away even though I have an accommodating parking spot out back in the alley behind the house. These math computations are also when I decided I liked Claire and Hank. They live downstairs in the basement apartment. Have so for the last six and half years. They have an arrangement with our landlord

Bettie. *Really no point, more of a hassle than anything to look elsewhere* – that's what Hank says. Claire's always good for a couple cigarettes for when Bettie stops by to check up on things, and Hank cuts the grass in the summer and shovels the walkway in the winter. So, rent has pretty much stayed the same all these years for Hank and Claire. Stuff like that is good for people like us. We deserve the break, especially them.

Our other neighbors in the rented house, below my apartment and above Claire and Hank, we could do without, but those apartment units never keep any tenants for long. We are not what the new neighbors are looking for in neighbors. Us three good neighbors take pride in that; it's our mutual bond. Before ever seeing or meeting us (Hank, Claire, and myself), young couples, or some drunk guy in his mid-twenties wanting to party, will rent units #2 and #3, assuming the other people, as in us, will be just as fun as them.

Everyone has different means of fun. That's a good thing. It's the necessity of checks and balances in order to keep the world somewhat sane. For instance, take Hank's idea of a good time, over the last 40 years of his life, the man has probably watched nearly 6,000 Los Angeles Dodgers games – not including the simulated seasons he manages during the offseason on his desktop and the countless hours spent in the online forum threads talking shop with other fans.

I like baseball as well. Sometimes, when I can hear him shuffling around out back, I'll throw on a baseball cap to take the garbage out. He doesn't immediately point it out, but in his roundabout way he always gets to the subject of baseball. The way Claire smiles at me between drags of her cigarette makes me think she knows I wear the hat on purpose. I'm interested in

Hank's ability to stomach an underperforming season by a favorite team. He has what it takes, I don't. I know there's a reason for that and I'm starting to believe I know how he does it. Most of all I like to hear out what he has to say about how life is going. Talking with him is better than any list of how to do life.

Years ago, while Claire was drunk on one glass of wine, she told me Hank spent two years in the service when he was 19. After putting in his time overseas, Hank didn't go home, though. He travelled, stayed with friends, took on seasonal work wherever he felt like living. Claire's mother had a bakery in Ireland. She doesn't run the business these days. I don't know if it was because of retirement or being forced to close shop due to finances. Either way, without fail, a couple times a year she mails Claire a box of homemade fudge, and then Claire gives the fudge to me.

Hank has never mentioned his family, but he likes hearing about mine. He tells of his friends' names in his recollections. They seem like interesting people, people I would get along with. Hank did not have fun at war, but he did meet Claire while stationed off the coast of Ireland; and, I know, by the way they share this here life, in space and time, this is how they do life. I like Claire and Hank, and I think they like me too.

Lucky Them

A guy killed himself in a cafe bathroom during hour two of forty-four of an open mic poetry session that he couldn't physically leave. Everyone in attendance was waiting to read; nobody was there to just listen. They all nodded constantly, accepting and agreeing with every single thing said.

They had locked the doors with chains, boarded up the windows, locked arms to form a human barricade, and didn't serve alcohol. And all the poems were about love and the weather and every word in every line in every poem was all just so grand, too funny, and so truly beautiful that he just couldn't take it anymore.

Floorboards

Of course I agreed, how could I not? Martin died when Eva, William, and Francis died out there on McKinley Road. The morning it happened, Martin phoned me to leave work and drive over. I remember how the point where two sides of a wall meet in the corner felt loud and how the edges of the table were sharp and unforgiving while he told me what happened.

A week later, after he buried the loves of his life, he asked me to take down the memories and box up the rest. I had a house across town with no wife or children that I lived in by myself; I had the room to store his life's tangible memories. I would keep the doors closed if he were to come over so he wouldn't have to see the boxes collecting sad, all organized and stacked in their own private rent free graveyard.

Martin was an over giving man, if he were to see how everyday his family's boxes sunk the floors of my house, he would demand he cover the cost of the floorboards caving in, so because of his generous persistence I never mentioned where I stored his family's belongings. Eventually I suspected Martin had an inclination they were behind the closed spare bedroom doors, so I put locks on the doors for him not to get in.

It was around late summer when I realized my house couldn't hold Martin's sadness any longer. Half of the house that was once above ground was now underground; the window above the kitchen sink that used to frame the maple tree out back was no more, the dirt from being 8 feet underground had shattered the window, the two story tall maple tree's roots reached across the floor. I was increasingly concerned Martin would start asking questions about my house's degeneracy, so I began spending late nights and early mornings shoveling out the dirt around the walls of the house. I would get to it while Martin wasn't around. I would have to be sure to distribute the dirt evenly across the property in order for Martin and the bank not to suspect something was a bit off. I was somehow nearing paying off the mortgage in full and didn't want to ruin things being so close and all.

As far as others, to hell with Ted. Ted is old and paranoid and my neighbor; digging out the house would surely get him going. I figured I may have to sign off on another loan, double up, buy Ted's mortgage off him. I began calling off work, using my sick days. It wasn't long, perhaps 3 weeks until I just stopped showing up for good. I wasn't concerned. I had 6 weeks of back pay still coming my way. No use for cable anymore, too much digging still yet to do. I'll call up the provider first thing tomorrow and cancel service; that ought to help some, in order to keep this thing going a little while longer.

Church Poem

Not being of such belief anymore, losing the vigor the young possess before one comes to terms with the law not caring if they throw you in jail or not, because if it isn't you, they will find someone else to take your place. I have now recognized my fragility in not wanting to answer the phone and certainly not the door. Afraid now of what and who might be there when it comes time to answer. What should I tell them this time? Regretting I had ever agreed in the first place back then.

What was once an unsaid knowing of something-is-happening-here with us in this place in time was already said by people who had already been. Even Eli seems to know it to be an aimless, dangerous joyride.

Look, I'm over here, sitting and watching from the orange painted chair in the corner, I'm not supposed to be here. My place should be some 1,100 miles off, bent on knees in a cold pew asking forgiveness while my mother waits out in the car with the heater on while it snows a Michigan snow, wondering why I am back home and not wanting to know what I have done.

War Time

My Dad's favorite time of the year is in the summer, when it's not too humid, and the Detroit Tigers are not losing. You gotta get him before it gets too hot, before he is forced to fork-over the money by turning on the AC. When this all comes together, my father is content with the world around him. It's usually some time between early June and early July when he tells me about that one time all over again, when he was 14 years old, him and his brother, my uncle Henry, taking a bus down to Detroit on the weekend of July 23rd, 1967.

It was a weekend getaway, which they often took from Kalamazoo to Detroit. It was a good way for them to learn how to get around and manage what little money they had. The greyhound would drop them off for one dollar and twenty-five cents at the corner of 12th and Clairmount on the city's west side. They would stay for free at the YMCA across the street and walk the half-mile to the stadium. Joe and Henry were to be there just for a weekend series vs. New York. This was before all the expansion teams, when no team was awarded a playoff spot unless you won damn near 100 games. It was a difficult time in baseball for the majority of teams' fans. The boys were excited though; through 93 games Detroit was in the race for the pennant. The Yankees at the time were long dead at 14 games back. Detroit was likely to win the weekend series so everyone in the city was sure to be in a good mood.

What the boys looked forward to most of all was walking around the city at night after the game. My dad told me it felt like the entire city was outside. My dad's brother would laugh and moan, stumbling down the streets pretending he was a pitcher who had blown out his arm by throwing 189 pitches. Sometimes it would garner some attention by way of the occasional person would ask him if he needed help.

Come late evening, 12th Street was a center for Detroit nightlife, with the city reluctant to call it a night by going home. It was the 1960s and people didn't want to go off to Vietnam. With brothers, friends, and old classmates trying to stay alive in southeast Asia, going home when the bar was supposed to close by city regulations meant possibly hearing bad news or not seeing that one guy at the end of the bar again because he may get his slip to report the next day. So, they hung out, held on, bought some time by telling and listening to another story.

Being teenage boys with a father who had served in the nation's previous war, Henry and Joe read history books about war and reenacted killing Nazis with the neighborhood boys by way of splitting up into good guys vs bad guys. The boys didn't play "Vietnam War" though. One of the neighborhood boys, Peter Clausin's older brother had been drafted and died in that same year of 1967. It was an unspoken agreed upon Peter was the top ranked officer for the good guys. And, boy, did he kill a lot of bad Nazis that summer. He turned into a killing machine, he would march the other boys who had a quarter of German blood out to the field behind the unused tennis court, and make them keep their eyes open while he shot them in the head with a wooden rifle bought from the corner drugstore. Pretend-killed or not, the boys liked the reenactment, it was a way for them to act brave for an afternoon's time when in truth they were all just young and scared.

In the late hours of Saturday night, early Sunday morning around 3 am on July 24th, Detroit police officers raided the weekend drinking club at 9125 12th St. arresting 82 black patrons who were celebrating the return of two local GIs. By midmorning, every policeman and fireman in Detroit was called to duty, and President Johnson was soon to call in the Federal troops. Jason Jones, 15 years of age, in the midst of the riots was sitting under a tree when he was shot in the chest. Often, people do what they are told by whomever or whatever pays their bi-weekly checks.

The city deemed it unsafe for the Tigers to play their home game the following Sunday afternoon, so the powers in charge moved the game to be played to their opponent's home field, leaving behind the players wives and kids. There were a lot of people down there carrying guns, my dad says. Says he saw a lot of cops with guns, but never saw any fellow citizens holding one. My dad had never seen an actual gun being fired off before, until then. He stopped playing pretend war in the neighborhood after that.

How to Organize a Neighborhood Block Party

I wish I lived with my family and friends all at once, simultaneously, but not in an overwhelming type of way. And, certainly not in the same house, like maybe some of them live on a nearby block and the rest would live across town, where I would have to take the city's train or a bus, but not a bus route that the city has extra buses for. No, it would need to be a bus that comes by once every 70 minutes or so. Also, it couldn't be in a city like Chicago with the train running 24 hours. Preferably it would be a city with on-and-off again weather, unpredictable, weather that can change in 10 minutes, that way I have the excuse of not meeting up on a Friday night.

Things to Do

I think I may die tonight, but I cannot. I live too far away from Mom and Dad. What about them? Not now, not yet. I wouldn't want it to be a hassle for Dad to drive the 1,000 miles out here to Colorado in the van, just to turn around and have to make the drive all over again. Sure, Dad likes running errands and having an excuse to get out of the house on a Saturday afternoon, however, this is different. To make a 60-year-old man drive through the states of Iowa and Nebraska, not once, but twice in one day? No way. I'm not selfish.

Such distance is tough on a van. Besides, Dad needs sleep and no hotel would allow me to stay the night. I still have things to do. I haven't made right with everything yet. I haven't paid back all my debts. I'm just starting to like who I am again. People who care about me are getting proud. I haven't coached little league baseball yet. Too much good music still to listen to and movies I haven't seen. I haven't lost my voice from screaming as loud as you can when you get really happy. I haven't told the people I love I love them enough. I still haven't witnessed my favorite baseball team winning the pennant in a bar with my best friend. There are still many more things to do.

Dead People Cannibalism

The bookstore was a used car lot, but not cars; not overpriced by a thousand and two dollars, but alike in supply and not being overly in demand. Seventy-six window shoppers on a July Christmas, thousands of 254 page novels and one or two used yellow page city directories. Not dead autobiographies, but not-yet-folded 1944 published paper airplanes. They came to the bookstore not for eye exercise, instead for already dead people cannibalism where the zookeeper doesn't keep, instead has unlocked the door and handed over the keys. And when the bookstore owner does happen to be there, he only looks up for a brief moment in between the period and the line.

Fragmentary Facts

Norman did things factually. He would figure out his personal shortcomings and do something to either rid himself of the situation entirely or make better of what was acknowledged before him. It is nice to have something or someone else to take the blame.

She was wearing the brown sweater he had purchased for her. It was the first week of September. The university's fall semester had just begun. She was enrolled, he wasn't. When they had first met it was his fifth semester and her second.

All the while, on a neglected farm, in an unvisited part of town, where the food production is nonexistent and the livestock has long since been sold off, there is a farmhouse with a screen door that no longer catches the frame. And, in that house, is where Norman decidedly stood, staring off at the dried out crop fields of nine years.

Norman had no wish to continue the debate with himself any longer. On that morning he selectively chose and pieced an outfit together that said, this is me, if I had one pair of pants and shirt to wear for the rest of my life, this would be it.

Norman decided that late morning he needed to rid himself of it, and then at last he did.

The History of Furniture and Wood Flooring in East Texas

The woods in Texas are in large part because of James Stephen Hogg. James Hogg was a great statesman in his day. When Governor Hogg asked back in 1906 that a pecan tree be planted at his place of burial, instead of the traditional cemetery headstone, it not only altered the perception and belief of what Texas is like, but also ramped up the state's opportunity to rival just about any state in furniture making.

For those who haven't visited Texas, people don't think of Texas as a place with a lot of trees. However, if one is to make their way through east Texas you are likely to have the thought or overhear a conversation about the abundance of the state's pecan trees. Texans talk about their land of trees in the way they talk about a local high school football star. Who would've thought?

The wood industry has its stake in the housing market, too, well, with just about every house you come across electing for wood flooring. It's good for the economy, keeping the flooring local and all. Provides steady work, one doesn't have to have a college degree to lay wood. My uncle Stephen does contract work, mostly home improvements, so he handles wood all day.

Aunt Carey used to drink a ton. It's part of the reason why she moved down to Texas, to get away from the influence of drinking buddies up in Michigan. Michigan is a great place for half the year, until it gets bitterly cold, then there isn't a whole lot to do besides hole up at a local bar down the street. The long winters bring about a proud we-are-in-this-together enduring feeling. People need human contact. Aunt Carey would have died the way she was drinking. We all die, I say.

Uncle Stephen never went to college, or maybe he did but called it quits after a class or two. Really I don't see why anyone would ever want that carpet stuff, that's what Uncle Stephen says. He has a point. Uncle Stephen and my aunt Carey are my godparents. Aunt Carey is my mother's sister, and closest sister of nine. As a teenager I wasn't bad-bad, but I did find some trouble with enough idle time and no parent supervision, so I spent three consecutive summers down in Texas with Stephen and Carey. It did me good getting away. Uncle Stephen put me to work and demanded I attend church. The church services were a bit odd; they had a feeling of everyone actively recovering from some sort of lifelong ailment. They had converted from Catholicism to non-denominational. That's fine. I just wasn't used to their constant smiling and hugging of each other.

Good on them and good on the governor centralizing all of this happiness and prosperity. With the governor's handling with always the state of Texas in mind, the pecan seed's worth came to be beyond pie and aesthetic pleasure. By way of using the wood from the trees, Texas entrepreneurs met opportunities over the years, like I said, in furniture and flooring, but that wasn't all, others capitalized by other ends, like in paraphernalia by way of their once-governor's legacy. In present day subcultures of east Texas, the woods people wear Hogg hats and t-shirts with Hogg's face printed on them, upholding his prominence in the Texas history books. Some even burn prayer candles like the 8" Virgin Mary of Guadalupe you can buy at a grocery store, but with Hogg's stately face wrapped around the glass instead of Mary's.

Big Jim, as his friends and admirers like to call him, consider their 20th governor a hero of Texas. Out near Tyler, TX, heading east on Interstate 20, they even named an exit 'Jim Hogg Rd'. And if you miss the exit, just 12 miles east there is a state park named after Hogg where you can camp on a first come first serve basis. Aunt Carey and Uncle Steve were married at the park. I was in the 6th or 7th grade when they had their wedding. It was a big deal when Aunt Carey married a direct descendent of the governor's bloodline. Aunt Carey at the time was 43-years-old when she met Uncle Stephen. Stephen and Carey met at a sober singles church bingo night. They hit it off right away by talking about their mutual deliverance from the world of sex, light drugs, and alcohol. During their vows Uncle Steve told everyone in attendance of their wedding how he knew Carey was the real prize of church sober bingo night and not the gift card to the church's bookstore they gave out to the other winner.

People go to the bars in Tyler to play Hogg Trivia and drink beer named after Hogg. Which explains the lack of non-Hogg related framed photos covering the walls of the bar. The bar has created quite the moral dilemma for Uncle Steve and Aunt Carey. Their church does other things besides hosting bingo; they also put on charity events, community potlucks, and anonymously burn down local bars in hopes of ridding sin and temptation. Uncle Steve is really having a good time with it all, he has always proudly stated he never cared for alcohol one bit. My mother told me about the recent bar burnings. She forwards the weekly church bulletins to me by way of Aunt Carey. Aunt Carey confides to my mother, telling her she isn't quite sure how to react to it all, in the meantime she asks for our prayers.

Self-Help

It occurred to him, at this moment, kneeling down in front of her on the bathroom tile, there was a choice. Things done could be forgiven. They could both move on, together. With the right attitude, they could pretend all of what happened didn't really mean much. They could start over again. If he were to say something, this was the time. But, she didn't want him to. He wasn't really taking care of her by cleaning up the wound, I mean, she could've put the alcohol on herself, but they both figured this would be remembered as their unspoken apology.

Drinking Whisky with Leon Trotsky Trout

Can't leave the apartment to take out the trash. Got the whole neighborhood asking me why I'm not at work. Neighbors down the way never go inside. They're from the south, just moved up north this past June.

"Everybody sits outside down there, always have."

Makes sense, I said.

Been waiting for a guy to come by for going on an hour now. Selling my air conditioner to him for a good price. Both of us win.

Being fired last week from my job got me thinking again. I was thinking about the grand scheme of things. I know this isn't new news, but we are all going to die and all we do is sleep and work. All we do. If only man was given time to think and pursue. Given such little time in between the time he is off work and at home and when he exhaustively falls asleep, there isn't much time there, is there? Perhaps three hours, four hours at best? I'm back from the dead this week. I've read three novels and had the energy to even exercise. Whatever happened to meeting at cafes, drinking strong coffee to talk and talk through the evening and night?

They don't want us doing that, do they? Otherwise, they may get nervous about us. Probably send one of theirs over here to listen in, to tell 'em what's what and who's who.

Then Raymond said, "Did you know less than 30 percent of history teachers in the country studied the subject in college? Also, I thought whisky had an "e" in it."

There ya go, I replied.

Both of the men now looking down.

Exactly.

All we do.

Local Weather

The summer will not die. It's out there in the backyard, on the tree, five inches under the surface of the ground. It's in the black trash bags full of cut grass that the door-to-door neighborhood lawn mower man for whatever reason stores in the woods. It's out there reflecting off the dozen bikes that were stolen from our block back in late June while all of our fathers were passed out drunk from the swimming pool party. It's in the way we walk and talk, us neighborhood boys scanning the blocks. Some of us even speak to one another about how perhaps we should start stealing things to make some extra money. It's out there in the loss of innocence.

It's there in the space created by the wind between your shirt and your stomach. It's in the color of Annabelle's shoulders and legs. It's still going fast out there on that two-way country road leading to the lake. It's heard in the choice of music being played in the next lane's car.

It's the reason why the kitchen windows haven't yet been cleaned. And why the college football game last Saturday seemed lighthearted, instead of competitive. Even the stolen flower in the Mason jar on the windowsill hasn't been thrown in the trash. And our dads think the baseball season has six weeks left, so none of us have been told to go to school. The whole neighborhood is like this, and the school hasn't bothered to call because they are in on it too.

Some of the neighborhood boys send me letters in the mail bragging about how they are still off at camp and should've been picked up two weeks ago. Rumor has it the girls' camp across the lake is talking to the boys' camp. A handful of us are pissed about it, so we are planning on borrowing some bikes to ride the 30 miles to camp come Wednesday to fall in love too.

before falling out of love

You both very much fell in love for 12 days. Which can lead people to make aggressive decisions about moving in together. And, with being of love, at the time, making it impossible of considering the not-in-love of ever occurring. Thereafter come the 78 half-days of being sort of in love. You were seduced by the nakedness of each other, and you convinced one another of the romantic idea of the next thing to do being moving away together to an expensive city on the coast. She deserving love, and an apartment in a neighborhood with restaurants you can walk to, believed you would take care of her needs and desires. During months one to four, before the not in love with you anymore time, you made love with her on the stairs leading up to the bedroom, at the park against the basketball court fence, in the backseat of her car at a rest stop in Missouri, in the laundry room of your parents' house on July 4th, and on the shoreline under that one tree at Lake Michigan.

you are:

The time – between, after, and before; a late afternoon 6-hours-later summit; the taste good waffles in bed makes; all the best wine I've ever had and will later have. You are: the big game is on but we are in the other room. You are: can't wait to see you again, I'm coming home. You are: me opening the door and you are there, then taking me out that very door I just walked through for me to see and think things I've never seen or thought before. You are: 5.5 liters of my body's blood rushing to my heart; you are: making it acceptable for me to even be somewhat okay with ever writing something like blood rushing.

acknowledging myself's mistakes

She is gone, but not gone-gone, just somewhere not here with me. She is off somewhere in this world, with someone else. To that other someone she is there with them, not yet gone. Where? I cannot say. Perhaps later she will decide to leave, or not. If I were not I, but somebody else, like a neighbor I don't know, or some person living in a city I do not live, I would say to her, how I would never do that to you like he did, as in me. I am not like him, he will say. Whereas I cannot say to myself the same.

The Evolution of All Things

A coat from another life, his father's oversized gray winter jacket with red inner lining hangs in the hallway closet. Josiah looks at himself in the mirror, combing his hair forward in failed attempt to deceive his aging to the rest of the world. Lately he has thought about moving away from the city, taking on a mortgage, and finding a 100-year-old house with wood flooring. After living and renting in a large city for nine years, anything but the city seems affordable in comparison. In a remote town he would cut his hair short, walk to the movie theater without wearing a ball cap to hide his thinning hair, and people would just assume he was nearing 40, instead of 30, and he would be fine with that.

With the delay and transfer in Cleveland, the train ride to Kalamazoo arrived late by two hours. Luckily there was daylight the entire ride through New York, in particular the stretch along the banks of the Hudson River, between New York City and Albany. The night and morning hours of the trip take you through Cleveland en route of Chicago, which isn't very scenic.

Normally a good son would find the soonest departing direct flight, but upon hearing of his father's fatal heart attack, his dad had already been dead. His mother would have called back a second and third time when Josiah didn't answer, but Josiah's sister, Marie, was phoning their mother on the other line just as she was about to make the second attempt to reach Josiah.

The next flight would make no difference; at least taking the train would allow him more time to think. He was a good son, despite those tough turmoil years of lashing out at his father over the dinner table. Their father-son relationship was healthiest when they didn't live in the same city.

His father's first heart attack occurred about the same time last year. The holiday time of year caused the family to come together even more as a family. In the hospital cafeteria they consciously appreciated each bite of food by reflecting on the ability to chew food. Josiah even thought about attending church for the first time since mandatory mass of his school years. He ended up not going and telling himself he would go next time; however, he did recite a few Our Fathers that night in the hospital. Since it had been some time, he had to look up the words of the prayers.

To make Christmas easier around the house this year without his father being around, Josiah bought a Pre-lit Fold-Flat Metal Christmas Tree at one of the nationwide retail hardware stores. It was durable, rust free, and came with a lifelong warranty replacement. To make it look not so much like a metal tree David painted the metal green. It didn't work. In order not to be questioned by the neighbors, Josiah's mother positioned the metal pointed object in the corner, away from the traditional location in front of the dining room window. Unless someone in the family has an allergy, resorting to an artificial Christmas tree is lazy and only somewhat acceptable if you reside in far off places like Tampa or San Bernardino. If Mom didn't want it around for next year, perhaps Josiah could take a drive up to Northern Michigan to plant it somewhere in the sparsely populated backwoods near Ishpeming and Marquette.

Josiah would take note in detail of what roads he turned left and right, mapping out where he had planted the tree. Perhaps with time, it would evolve out of survival, rooting itself like its surroundings, taking on a new identity in life.

The funeral was attended by their loving, quiet family. Leaving the ceremony, Josiah is wearing the winter coat of his late father. The son has brought the winter coat a new life. It is not the winter of 1973, when his father first wore it, yet the winter weather is just about the same as then.

Back in 2003 when watching four TV shows in a row was considered an insane amount of TV watching

On Saturday afternoons I would go with him to the empty office downtown; I asked him what an employee time punch clock was. He had an unlimited supply of legal pads he took from the office storage room. The yellow paper gave whatever I listed a sense of authenticity. I would list my friends in the 3rd grade, my top 3 favorite numbers, songs I liked on the radio, and a list of fun things to do. Dad sold property insurance to farmers. At the office he set out Paydays and Mars candy bars in an old card box on the counter in the employee lunchroom and charged 50 cents. At the end of the week he would give me what little money was collected from the honor system.

Dad went to a sporting goods store to buy a baseball tee and instead gets pissed off about the price. He rigged up a PVC pipe in the yard for the neighborhood boys and I to whack at with the designated metal bat one of us kept in the garage.

Dad and I went to the grocery store only at night. How wise. I used to think the families that had more money shopped in the afternoon, giving them first pick. Dad and I were a different breed: we bought the leftover bruised fruit and knew the meat would go on discount 20 minutes before closing time.

Dad had an old 1950s bomb cellar, when bomb shelters were all the rage. The cold brick cellar turned into a hangout and was covered in late 1960s Playboy nudes after everyone realized the Russians weren't coming – my first lesson in sex.

Arriving home from school one day, I asked Dad, *Why home so early?* It was just after three in the afternoon and he had already put on his green bathrobe he bought for himself as a Christmas present a couple years back. He watched a lot of rerun television in those two years. Spaghetti with Wonder Bread that acted as garlic bread was a frequent family dinner while Mom worked till midnight managing Hudson's department store. It made a lot and was easy to make. I had learned the world wasn't always fair for the good guys. My dad was no longer just a dad. I felt his vulnerability. He needed my help.

Waiting out in the van, stretched out in the backseat, Dad tells me to stay put, that he wouldn't be gone long.

Dad's friend built a cabinet for him as his final project before he died of cancer.

Dad took me to my first baseball game: 1993, 2121 Trumbull Ave, Detroit, Michigan. 52,436 fans chanting a player's name in the streets in the heat of summer while we all file out to head on home.

This is your future self telling your old self that you gotta be there, you just can't miss it

Your little brother is about to recite Ginsberg's Supermarket in California poem. He has been practicing for a long time. For Christmas he even wrote it down on his list: Complete Collection of Ginsberg's Poems.

Sweet. So, where are you? He thinks you are just running a little late, that you are on your way, perhaps stuck in traffic. He can only stall for so long before his 9th grade English teacher tells him the show must go on, the judges can't wait any longer.

C'mon, man, tell whoever you are with that you gotta go because you love that poem too and you love your little brother even more. Man, you gotta be there, you can't miss it. Because no offense but whatever the hell you were up that night wasn't even fucking close; so unless you have figured out a time machine that will allow you to go back in time over and over again to that given night at that specific moment, then it's over, go say to your future self, go fuck yourself.

Detroit Hustles Harder

It's cold out and it has been since the second week of October. It's Michigan, deal with it. The city is coming together. People are saying hello to passing strangers, the tap water is drinkable again, and all the jobs are coming back to the city. There's a feeling in the air that all the wrongs and injustices may just balance out after all, and maybe, just maybe we aren't all totally screwed. The cause for this renewed vitality is in part due to baseball. The Detroit Tigers are finally the odds on favorite for winning the World Series; but for this October they end up playing all the games on the road in the opposing team's city. Real tough break. Probably the first time in baseball World Series history a team has been forced to do something like that. There's just too much snow, too cold. The local weather station stopped showing up for work because we already know what's what. Good for them, I would do the same.

Everyone is calling bullshit. They have a point. They play football and hockey out in the snow, so for once, why not try baseball? Let's see how it would go, we want to see the action. The fans are irate, and most of the players are too. I like seeing the baseball players get angry about it – makes them more humanlike. Even though I grew up in Michigan, I don't particularly root for the home team, but this time I do. For four whole games I cheer and pray, and then I pray some more. Yeah, I pray that hard. I pray for them to win because all my family wants them to win, big time. I buy into the hype: World Series Time. Naturally, I lay serious money and then some. I'll overdraft on my bank account if they lose. No worries, not a concern. I know the game of baseball, they can win – I even read *The Complete Encyclopedia of Baseball* 2013 Edition.

Damn. In the end not much worked out. They lost all four games. Wow. What a game. 162 regular season games, and if your team is lucky enough, they get to play some more in the playoffs. Tougher on the players or the fans? Impossible to quantify, both are invested. My mom says the team played hard and there's always next year – she always says that, it's comforting. Thanks Mom. My little brother, sort of like a Moneyball-dude-guru, knows all the baseball stats and is riddled by the outcome of the season – it just didn't add up. My Dad doesn't say anything, he is in utter disbelief. I say things to make him feel better about it, to lessen the blow. I remind him of the city's ex-mayor and how he's locked up in prison for the next 30 years. A man can't get away with stealing from his own people, this makes my dad smile a little. I tell him to call in sick for work tomorrow, but he doesn't, he shows up 2 hours early at his desk the very next day. He won't mention anything about the games; he will act like it never happened for a week or two. Then one day, he will come home from work and let the whole neighborhood know, and the cashier at the grocery store, and the church priest, and the mailman, and everyone. I feel real bad about it all. A win would've made the family happy.

Mom tells me about when her and my dad moved out of the apartment and were in the process of purchasing the family's first home, they drove around four or five different neighborhoods in the city to see where they wanted to raise a family. The house they decided on was the oldest and smallest of all their options. They went with the house because the other houses they considered putting bids on were too spacious for my mother's liking. She says she wanted to feel like everyone was home.

I like our living room because it's smaller than most, everyone has to cram in and sit right next to one another. It was nice to watch baseball in the living room with the family. It felt good to get that close.

Guide to Rooftop Sleeping in the City

A lot of times we would walk over to the park with a case of beer, some hot dogs, and a bag of chips to spend the afternoon drinking and eating. It was great entertainment. It was a way to get out of the house. It helped the beer was noticeably inexpensive, it was a limited-edition specialty beer that they brought back from the 1970s: same color, label, and taste. They even stuck with the same price. Probably the same damn beer and kegs, too.

"Look, they used a quarter on the bottom to scratch off the expiration date!" That's what my friend Russell would say. I laughed every time.

I'm a good person to tell a joke to. Russell tells me it's one of his favorite things about me.

The beer was cheap and we found a way of making money while drinking it. In only two hours time we would make enough money to cover the cost of the case and food. There was a river that cut through the park, and often people would set up on the banks for the day, lounging, swimming, drinking. Unfortunately, by way of human recklessness, cans of beer would be swept in and sunk to the bottom. This being the case, Russell and I helped out by swimming up and down the river, diving and coming up with handfuls of waterlogged beer cans.

We received 10 cents for every can we brought to the recycling center.

Some other friends found Russell to be annoying, repeated the same lines, told the same stories, that sort of thing, but I didn't mind. Deep down I think he knew he was saying the same things. Maybe he saw it in a movie or something, thought reminiscing over and over the same stories is what good friends are supposed to do. Sure, why not. He's probably right; anyways, I remember him more because of it.

One time we brought home some leftover beer to Russell's father's house and he flipped. Russell's dad is really into history. He hadn't seen the brand in over 30 years, so it was a real mind-bend. Apparently back in the day it was a cheap beer all the college kids drank. Said you had to nearly drink a dozen of them to feel anything. We laughed when he said that. He was a real nice man. Russell's father died a couple years ago. His camera and photography collection was immense. Of course he left them all for Russell.

Russell likes to tell the story about the summer we decided to see how many different roofs we could sleep on. He kept count by setting up his camera and timing a photograph of us two standing side-by-side with his arm draped over my shoulder on every roof we stayed on. We slept on 24 roofs. Russell kept track by numbering the back corner of each roof photograph we took together. Friends, local businesses, once atop our favorite bar, and one time a stranger's, all unknown to everyone. We made a summer of it.

I don't see Russell much anymore. Last time I saw him was when I drove up north for a weekend to check out his new house. The house is perfect for him. Old, enough rooms, and of course a perfect top window allowing him access to the roof. I since moved across the country, and he has a family with a wife, two kids, and a third on the way. A good life.

It's not like I've lost all connection with him though. Once in a while, when he has had two or three beers, he will call me up late at night. Most of the time he just wishes to say hello, to tell me about his new neighbors, his job, but sometimes when he calls he doesn't say anything about any of that, instead he holds out his phone for a minute or two, to the air, to have me listen. He wants to remind me. I know where he is.

Dead Banana

You didn't say goodbye and you didn't think of taking a banana from the kitchen counter – you're going to be hungry out there on the road. You could've grabbed the clock from the wall on your way out, now I have to eat it.

when the water runs out

It's the future, but it's happening at this moment, which is leading to the future. In the not far off there's very little accessible water left. Over the last couple decades, a handful of corporations have been extracting and then selling off all the reservoir and lake water: The Great Lakes, the Colorado River Basin, Millard Canyon in California, just to name a few. The corporations have decided water should go to the highest bidder. Buyers are reaching out all across the world. People have become nervous.

My friend Tony only makes 11 dollars an hour as a food runner at Applebee's, how do they expect him to buy this new way of water? Some friends and I are going around town collecting reserve water just in case the rivers and lakes in the area go completely dry. We are strategically placing buckets around town and asking people if they would be willing to give us their spare bathtub to use for filling up rain water. We show them our ladders; we tell them we would be happy to carry the bathtub up to their roof. We are trying to save our town. It's difficult, but we think we can do it if enough people join us. We don't want to have to move to the big city where all the water pipelines have gone. We like it here.

A week passes; more people donate bathtubs and buckets. I think some of the people just want to actually see us try hauling a bathtub up a ladder. Tony is no longer working at the restaurant; instead he's now helping us full-time with our water efforts. He told me he got fired for not claiming all of his tips. Tony shows up the next day on his bicycle carrying two ladders. He starts telling all of us about these documentaries he watched last night. We are pumped. His new energy keeps up the morale. It's just like old times. All the friends are together and everyone knows we are coming.

Some of the neighbors are a little scared to open their doors, they aren't quite sure of our new activist approach. Some of us are loud and have nothing and everything to lose. We station a member of our group at every public pool in town to guard against any outside corporations with nefarious plans. We hear they are coming our way. The rest of us keep knocking on doors to spread the word. For the people who don't answer their doors, we leave the complete anthologies of Edward Abbey and John Muir on their doorsteps. That will keep them busy. Huge success, everyone who reads the books either lights themselves on fire or joins the water cause.

We keep at it, we are relentless, I call up Gary Snyder and tell him I love his poems, especially the ones where he rages about the beauty of water. I ask him if I can give out his poems for free. He says yes. Says he will come out and help the cause. Gary says he is bringing some friends and ghosts with him, old revolution/poet type of friends who died long ago. Cool. I tell him I have a good friend out his way in Oregon who loves the water poems too; I ask if he would be willing to pick him up along the way. Sure, sounds good, no problem, he says – Gary has a huge bus he has been renovating over the last year. I get off the phone and tell all the friends that Gary is coming and he's about to make it rain. My friends and I throw a huge block party with all the good food and music you can think of.

Where the air tastes better, colder, cleaner

There's a window of about twelve days in September, when all the birds come out in full swing, dominating the sky, flying overhead, with each second producing more and more birds, thousands and thousands of them by the second, in peak southward migration. It all builds up. Soaring powerfully, effortlessly. It's the most beautiful sky you've ever seen in all of your lives you've ever lived. Depending on the desired route, stopovers, wind current, and how they are feeling, the duration of the migration varies by months. Freedom. Some fly high, some fly low. Some get going; others leave at the last minute. My friends and I come to watch them every September. We are out here, together, standing on the overpass, flopping and jumping, trying to feel what it would be like where the air tastes better, colder, cleaner. It's the closest we'll ever get. Meanwhile cars below drive by wondering what in the world we are doing.

Georgia

My friend was playing his part up in the driver's seat by not settling for a mediocre song on the radio. He would never settle for that. He was a madman who could be trusted with everything and nothing. He was an angel and devil.

Where was I going? Why Georgia? May as well been anywhere. I wanted to be away from the comfort and known of home. My friend said let's go, so I go. With my body contorted in the backseat, I watched the warm black Kentucky countryside pass the window in a continuous frame with an ever so often-distant barnyard light indicating whoever was in charge to change the reel because someone out there was watching. I felt directionless, yet moving towards something, beyond my knowing. I felt without God and with God more than ever.

It must've been two or three in the morning by now and we were the only people on the road. Perhaps we had fallen asleep at some hour in there and had already died a couple hours ago from driving off the road but we just didn't know it. Either way, we hadn't seen traffic for what seemed like 200 miles. I didn't want more coffee. I didn't want to sleep; I had done enough of that for a lifetime. What else was there to do in early March with the Michigan wind blowing snow into everyone's house? Long ride to go. I bet it will be nice country down there, but I sure couldn't see it, not yet, not then. I was idly hauling across America, half asleep, half awake, with very little idea of what I was doing and where I was going, putting my trust into something.

Holiday Pears

In line at the post office he smiled, while the children just ahead in line with their father, chased each other by running circles around the holiday display boxes that showed how your flat cardboard was to look prior to your arrival at the shipping counter. While waiting and shifting weight from one foot to the other, half of the neighborhood patrons in line would be inconveniently putting together their one size too large or too small box.

A dashed list penned on the backside of an envelope was healthy for William; it provided a sense of tangible doing. Pressed with black ink gave a feeling of urgency and purpose for the day. His favorite part of this system was when he would strike through whatever he got done, indicating he was getting on with his afternoon. Holding a box of delicious holiday pears, William wondered if the brown tiles he shuffled on, in his brown loafers, were the original tiles that dated back to the construction of the building, probably so. William liked the building's ornate charm.

In the hardship of the holidays, having no family that ever bothered to visit, William would bravely half-smile to people he came in contact with; soon he would have to smile for the post office clerk and tell her everything is good and well with his life. It was 2 o'clock and he was soon to be in his third conversation of the day. William did his best, but worried he wouldn't be able to keep it up forever. This was to be the tenth year in a row spending Christmas once again alone.

Somewhere behind him in line, an elderly woman spoke up about the change in weather, and how it was supposed to snow come early evening. Five of the nine people in line acknowledged her observation with an agreeing nod. Five out of nine was a good number. William was one of them. In the past he had tried this technique before, occasionally a stranger would entertain his attempted engagement, but never at a rate of above 50%, like the woman just received. Looking about, he figured the other four who didn't respond, probably would have reacted in similar fashion if they hadn't been miscalculating box sizes. She received about 60% feedback, could've been 100% if it weren't for the awkward boxes. Talking about the weather helps; there is a togetherness in the weather. William figured this topic could be a good starting point for his upcoming conversation with the clerk. William was soon to be next in line.

Finding North

You told me one night you were going to leave. I'll find a way, you kept saying over. Do you want to come, too? you asked. We can go to the mountains, find a nice spot with a good view. No one goes there anymore.

Yeah?

Yeah.

That sounds nice.

There was a river that cut through town, you and me 20 feet above, scaling the train tracks. No one else knew you were leaving for good in the morning. I pretended like I didn't know and you pretended like you didn't know I was pretending. You had a map on your wall marked up of the places you wanted to go. We must have walked north on those tracks for six hours that night. I knew you had to leave, but part of me thought if we just kept on walking that maybe you would forget that you were leaving in the morning. Perhaps we would come to a small town, some 50 miles away from here, and you would think this place seems just fine to start over new. We both know I wanted to go with you. We could send word to back home that we were off to find The Great White Whale.

I remember when we were little, Dad telling us about what it was like before: Birds, birds that actually flew and chirped and chattered.

Remember?

I tried to imagine what it would be like. I had seen a photo once, but that was a long time ago.

Birds of America

The mountains are shrinking and the birds of America are just too sad about it to wait around and watch it all happen, so they gotta go. It's truly a sight to see. I want to yell up to the sky and talk with them. I want to hear their take on all of this, and not just about the mountains but also about the pesticides and overdevelopment of infrastructure, but they can't hear me, they can only see me waving and jumping up and down from below. They are leaving by the minute, trying to go establish home elsewhere with bird relatives and bird friends across the way, but there is a giant glass window that keeps rising every day. You can't see the glass window from here, it's a ways out from town, but at certain parts of the day, like real late at night or early in the morning, when most people haven't woke yet, you can hear the sound it makes.

Goodbye Jim Harrison

Where are you now? Because I know even a dead man floats. You nearly outlived us all. You stuck it out when others gave in, and you came out on the other side. Is it warm enough for you? You never could quite decide which weather you liked best. Michigan, Arizona, Montana: Cold, hot, somewhere in-between. Wherever you are I bet they have good food. You should've been a chef, but you decided to be a poet. Just about the same. Your poems could make a broke man rich and a rich man fall to his knees to lick the dirt. Man, you could make any dad in America like poetry. You're the Trout Fishing in America Poem King. Where are you, Jim? With your wife whom you wrote about with love? Send us a signal. Here, here is a totally uncontrollable river for you to watch over and keep an eye on. Send us a signal. There you are. Here is something beautiful. Man, Jim, you're so good you could make a blind man see.

Drink Pop with Mao

Day 4 or 5:
I can't see Denver in the distance, so by now we must have started heading southwest, northwest, north, or south – not sure at this point, either way I'm out for now and won't be heading back to the city for a bit. Could be months or weeks on account of us having such a time.

The last couple days had me thinking about life. Something quite wonderful happens when you allow yourself to drift through life without a plan of direction. It feels as if all my late decided actions in life all finally made sense when last week I found myself well past the marked trail and still out hours later than I anticipated. With only an hour's sunlight left to find the trail again, and being some 8 miles from the parking lot, it made sense to find a good spot to sleep till morning. It didn't take long before it started to rain though. Deciding to seek more suitable shelter, I came to a small cave where another human happened to be living. He appeared to be well fed, despite his worn clothing and abnormal living arrangements. He's the other person who makes the "we", Mao and me that I mentioned above. I know, it's wild, huh. Mao in flesh, alive, still! I haven't asked him yet how he has defied the existence of time by surviving all these years, but I'll make sure to get around to the secret before heading home.

For now, we are simply enjoying one another's company. The world out here is quite mysterious. It is powerful – with the right mindset and intentions, it can bring forth a world of incomprehensible ways. I don't know if it is because of the combination of high elevation and too much sun in Colorado, but the nature world and one's mind is very thin. Of course, when I say "out there", I really don't mean that. Truly there is no out there or exterior world and interior world that is excluded from the other. At campfire last night, Mao said something that stuck with me.... for the individual to change, so too the world changes. For you to not change, the world will not either. That's just the way of it. Living is dangerous. Go on.

Day 6:

During Mao's reign he slept about 4 hours a night. I didn't ask how he managed, but after an hour of silently staring at each other over breakfast, he spoke up telling me he sleeps more now. Due to frequent heart attacks in the 1970s he started limiting his amphetamine intake. He told me a philosopher, visionary, poet, and military strategist of his ability couldn't be bothered with inferior habits like sleeping in or planning weekend brunch. Time changes a person though. The new Mao, as he refers to himself, is casual, takes a lot of small naps. As far as any planning goes, it's still deliberate from his end, but good intentioned and free going. New Mao told me he doesn't believe in the concept of time anymore like he used to. He said in his past his obsession of running out of time was what drove his decisions minute-by-minute. He is just living good and healthy these days.

Day 7:
Sun up. Sun Down. A lot happens if you look close enough. You earn your days out here. We develop a routine. This routine feels rather instinctual, like you've done it before. It becomes simple quick. You like doing it. A day feels like a day ought to. Two hours is two hours. They say you begin to find your rhythm around the 60-hour mark. The first 24-36 hours are spent on your brain catching up, processing your recent actions. Thereafter, a calmness, a peace comes about, a giving in, to you being out there and here you are. Your dad very well could have just won the lottery, but out here, you wouldn't know.

Day 8:
You can't force it, he says. He doesn't have a definitive name for this it. I trust him, so I go along with it. It's not weird or anything, it's basically just sitting. We let "it" come to us, whatever that it is, I'm not sure. The it comes and goes. Mao's really good at keeping it around for longer than I am. My back usually starts to hurt around the 20-minute mark until I find a nearby tree to lean against. Mao sits still for an hour, no problem. I think about things, but mostly I look at Mao, wondering what he's thinking.

We are getting low on food supply, so I holler on down to Mao telling him I'm going back into town to buy us food and snacks. He asks if I can bring back some pop. Sure, pop rocks.

Day 8 (afternoon):
By some freak phenomenon the corner market back in town shelves Faygo pop. Not only that, they have all the flavors in supply, so I buy a case of each flavor because I can't decide

between one over the others. While paying at the counter, I notice the clerk has a computer and printer hookup going on in the backroom. I ask him for a favor, if it would be okay for me to print something off – just a couple of pages, no big deal. Sure, why not, he replies. I find articles, blog posts, Buzzfeed lists, and official Yelp Reviews about Faygo, to bring back to Mao. Mao enjoys random facts like me.

Day 8 (evening):
Mao says for every can of pop you drink, you should have a glass of water, so not to rot your teeth. Fair enough. Mao tells me he thought about being a dentist, but history had other plans. My mother went to school to be a dentist, but then she met my dad at a bar the night Magic Johnson won a National Championship for Michigan State University. Thanks to fate and timing, my parents got married. To think, a glance, a minute later, a decision different, and I never would've been given the opportunity to be a son, root for Michigan State, or casually drink pop.

I hope I get to live as long as Mao. He says you get better at life with more time. Not all people do, but I like to think most of us will.

Dead Bird

Just saw a car run over a bird, and every poem written by the human race laser beamed up to the sky, carrying the bird with it. The car and the person kept driving though, as far as I know, they are still here with the rest of us.

If I could do it all over again

If I could do it all over again I would go back and say hello to more passing strangers. I would establish myself as a friend who picks up the phone and responds every time with a straight answer, even if it meant saying difficult things and telling the truth when I necessarily didn't want to, and people would respect that. I would go see more of those special feature movies that are only shown for 3 to 5 days max at your local theater, because I can never find them online to watch or rent. I would say yes more. I would worry less about the things I worry about. I would be more courageous. I would eat more vegetables. I wouldn't sit so close to the television. I would spend all my money on birthday presents for my family and friends. I wouldn't be so embarrassed about certain things. I would be proud. I would probably watch fewer sports. I would be kinder; I would kill them all with kindness. I would be grateful. I would use all the words, every last word to tell you. I would leave nothing off the page. I would write and write some more, and when I filled up all those pages to tell you, I would take the bus to the store to buy some more paper. Then I would read all of it to you. If I could go back, I would ask if it would be okay if I brought over a handheld audiocassette recorder to record the first time we told each other I love you. I would have that audio recording now, and I would listen to that short seven-second clip to hear what it felt like to have someone love you.

according to your preference

The trees are ancient new-aged telephone poles not serving anyone in the telephone kind of way. More so in the, everything-else-can't-live-without-you, type of way. And here's another thing about them, they are all in the same business and none of them work or compete against one another. It's everything businesses are not. They are check out all the books from the library to find the exact love passage in order to explain how you are feeling on that specific day. Even more, they are highlight the lines for your lover to see because maybe you can't physically talk anymore, or maybe don't want to, deciding this way just fits you more, type of way.

Dead Fish

Since corporations are killing off all the fish, good thing we all like pizza. Let's have a party, America. I'll bring some of those dollar store party hats, you bring the pizza; afterwards we can take a walk through the cemetery. Are we having fun yet? Where's the garage party at tonight? Those were always good. These parties suck nowadays. I don't even want to go. I'm not going to answer my phone when they call. Fuck off. Maybe in a couple years, when we all get sick of pizza, we will get angry enough to start that revolution everyone has been going on about.

Hoop Dreams

It was 1998 and Dennis Rodman was our favorite basketball player. Everybody loved Michael Jordan and Scottie Pippen, they were the best, that was easy. We liked Dennis best because he was a freak and his jump shot was ugly. At the park we played our game like Dennis Rodman: purposefully missing shots in order to accumulate more rebounds on the stat sheet, diving on the concrete for loose balls, temporarily dying our hair for a day with green and red Kool-Aid, you know, Rodman type of stuff.

My neighborhood friend across the street, Bill, even tried to talk like him. Bill would listen to recorded sideline interviews of Rodman and Craig Sager on replay for hours. Bill was two years older than us, so we usually went along with what he told us. I didn't really think about girls at the time, but Bill liked them, so the rest of us started noticing them as well. We liked Rodman because he dated Carmen Electra. She was on the hit American action drama series about the Los Angeles County Lifeguards *Baywatch.* Dennis wasn't considered good looking, so it gave hope to all of us teenage losers that we could date one of the *Baywatch* babes, too. We all thought we were inevitably destined for the NBA, that was a given, but Dennis dating a television supermodel was an added boost of confidence.

We loved *Baywatch* almost as much as basketball. We would watch *Baywatch* after NBC Saturday afternoon Chicago Bulls games. Bill would tape the episodes of *Baywatch* and the

Chicago Bulls games and then make VHS mixtapes for the 20 boys in our neighborhood to watch. The mixtapes would usually start off with a slow-motion of our favorite lifeguards running down a stretch of coastline, followed by an emphatic two-handed Chicago Bulls slam dunk. Bill's family was the first family on the street to own a computer. They had a fricking original iMac. Bill was a legend.

June of 1998 was the last time we ever saw Bill. The Chicago Bulls defeated the Utah Jazz in the NBA Finals on the night of June 14, and a couple weeks later the legendary Bulls dynasty broke up. Dennis Rodman left Chicago and signed a contract with the Los Angeles Lakers, probably to be closer to the *Baywatch* set, and Bill's family moved away at the end of the month to Alaska after Bill's mother won a jackpot at the Gun Lake Casino. It all happened so quickly. It didn't make sense to us that people would move away once they got a little bit more money. The following year, with failed contract negotiations, the NBA players and team owners entered a lockout, suspending the start of the basketball season. Upon hearing word of a postponed NBA season, us kids burned our Dennis Rodman jerseys in the driveway and didn't bother with anything Los Angeles TV related. It had become all too unrealistic, none of us had ever been west of Minneapolis, and what did we know about surfing and the ocean, anyways. The summer of 1998 was ending, giving way to fall of 1998. Soon two more families moved away. The neighborhood was changing, us with it.

Dead Deer

Twenty miles outside of Santa Fe, seven wild, now still horses, surround a just dead deer, while we all drive by wondering if we could have done something to stop all the killing.

Davis's Time Theorem

In the car Davis adjusts the passenger seat so that he is practically lying down bed-style. I glance over and his palms are across his eyes to shade against the evening sun. It has been in the 90s for the last couple weeks, or maybe it has been a full month now, either way the sun feels brighter than usual. Davis keeps me up on the news; he is really into Chaos Theory, The Butterfly Effect, Government Controlled Weather Operations, and all that type of stuff. Lately his new thought is how to slow-down time itself. I like when he tells me the news from all the articles he reads. Last week he convinced me the sun is going to swallow the earth whole. Better get living.

I have agreed to live with him in his RV. I just finished studies at the university, and have no job, so why not. Davis is pretty smart. Davis used all of his savings from working construction 60 hours a week for the past three years to purchase the RV. The weekend of his 21st birthday I drove with him to Wisconsin to buy it from some guy he found in a newspaper ad. We sleep in unattended parking lots across America. Minus gas money to and from, it's free rent, which allows us to spend our money on other things we care about. The past week we have been staying at this grocery store parking lot where the employees hangout and party with us on their lunch and smoke breaks. It's real chill.

Davis makes his money sports gambling online. Days when he wins some money are even more enjoyable. Even when he loses it is fine. Tomorrow is another day he tells me. He usually spends just about all of the winnings in a day's time. On days when he wins a lot we go all out. We give some away to random people we meet, like some of the grocery store employees, because they get paid shit.

Don't worry; he isn't an addict or anything. Davis and I could stop all of this and head home if we wanted. We do it because we like each other's company. Sure, the fun of it all keeps us going, but most of all we like being together. We are best friends. We know we will one day have our own families to spend the majority of our time, go on RV trips with, etc.

When you first meet a special person, you want those initial days, weeks, moments to last almost forever. The best is when we are in those moments and know when it is happening. All the driving and camping has slowed life down some. Whenever we stop at a library for some Internet time, Davis prints off all the articles he can find on how to slow down time, meditation, and the theory of relativity. He has taped them all over the inside panels of the RV. I think he knows I am thinking of moving to Colorado when we get back from this trip. I haven't officially told him yet. At first I didn't understand why he avoided the highways, but now I get why he is choosing the long way home. We know our time together, right here right now, won't go on forever, so we are holding on as hard as we can, trying to make it last a little longer. We all have our ways of doing this, this just happens to be ours.

Dead Jack Kerouac

Forgot how it goes, but that one Jack Kerouac quote before he gave up and taught us how to live, when he was headed west, at the dividing line of the east of his youth and the west of his new life, crossing over the state line of Colorado into Utah, seeing God in the sky above the desert salt in the form of a giant, magnificent sun, with all that road ahead and all that road behind, pushing and pulling with one's life at the center of it all.

3 minute and 34 second story at 8:13 in the morning

The day had promise of rain things, middle of the week wake up to morning rain in bed type of things. To their luck, today was that type of day – it was about to rain. On rain days like today they would call in sick to Mr. Bossman, telling him, not possible, no way could they make it in, not-going-to-happen.

They had only 3 minutes and 34 seconds to make it from the front doorstep to the 3 by 3 foot spot where they liked to stand. She loved him and he loved her. Now there were less than 41 seconds remaining to get from their apartment stoop to the 3 by 3 foot spot I just previously mentioned. They spent 27 seconds putting on their rain jackets and rain boots. It didn't rain much where they lived, but this morning was different, they could tell it was about to pour.

Time was ticking. They eagerly rushed down the sidewalk, turning left, then right, up just two more blocks, then, there, there it is on the left, at the corner. With only 3.3333 seconds remaining they arrived at the 3 by 3 foot spot under the cafe's awning, where they liked to hold hands and stand in their favorite spot, even more so when it was raining.

because maybe more is less

Ontonagon, Michigan, just down the road. A way of life. They don't have a lot of what you have and it doesn't bother them because, for most things, you can't miss what you never had.

Their water comes from the mile walk down to the Ontonagon River, pales in hand. When it rains they put out pots and pans. In winter they boil the snow.

Everywhere there's air, trees, and water.

If it gets too hot, they jump in the river and see how long they can hold their breath. If it gets cold they sit by a fire. On perfect nights they sleep with just one sheet.

And the girls talk beautifully, and the boys have deep voices for 12 year olds, and the adults only use words everybody understands.

Pete and Pete

The nuns at school would put on *Rudy* when they were hungover and didn't have any Friday lesson plans. After our school's one VHS copy broke from watching it one too many times, they lined us up and ordered us into a large carpeted room where we would run sprints back and forth for hours, training to be like Rudy. It was sort of like one of those padded rooms at psych wards, but extended, long and narrow, and with hard carpet on the floors and walls.

I never got to be Rudy, though. I was too tall and skinny; I was more like Rudy's best friend, Pete. Maybe you've seen the movie. The Pete character died from an explosion while working the graveyard shift at the mill – it usually pays 50 cents more an hour, so it's totally worth it. What a lower-middle-class-Midwesterner way to go out. Poor guy, died too young, and in Indiana of all places. You only want to die in a place like Indiana if you are from Indiana, even then.

Who knows how many recesses we had as kids. Certain days it felt like most of the school day. I don't remember much adult supervision when we were out there on the playground. One kid's mom, I bet, but she couldn't keep a watchful eye on all of us. During religion class we would sit in our seats in rows, arms reached out across aisles towards your fellow equal, praying out loud in unison, but outside of the classroom we didn't behave as such.

The school didn't have an air conditioner and still probably doesn't. Starting from the beginning of the day, our stringent dress code of formal wear, including a tie, made us scratchy and irritable. At lunch, some kids ate better lunches than others, which made some of us start questioning things. Why this, why that? A social order had begun to form and we were beginning to know of our place in line.

At first, I wanted to be more like Rudy. I wanted to be on the front lines. That's where all the action was. I wanted people to know and chant my name like they did for Rudy in the movie. However, that wasn't to be.

Being more like Pete resulted in being left out in the middle of the field, whereas Rudy would meet head-on in a tackling fest with the other Rudys. I was quiet and preferred to sit in the back of the classroom, going unnoticed; like in that one scene when for 1.52 quick seconds the camera zooms in showing Pete in the back corner of the class, writing something in a notebook of some sorts. What was he writing?

Years later, one night in the fall semester at the university, without any sort of direction or plan, I wandered into a lecture hall to this wild-haired old man talking to twenty students about the rise of the workers and the need to fight the fight for fellow Petes. I found it all very interesting so I stuck around and hung out afterwards. We all ended up going over to this dude's house across campus to talk and drink coffee and jugs of wine for a week straight. It was exciting.

Okay, very well, I was a Pete. I ended up liking being a Pete. It came to be that a lot of my friends I inevitably congregated with later on in the formative years were also Petes. One of those Pete friends I met in college lent me a Pete book by

Upton Sinclair, *The Jungle*, it made me like Pete even more. Upton Sinclair and the Chicago meatpacking workers, the young children, and the mothers and fathers, who were too old to still be working in the factories, were Petes, too. Pete, Pete, Pete. Pete had history. Pete was a true underdog. It felt good to be a Pete with the rest of them. I had become a full-blown Pete in mind, body, and soul. Long live Pete.

The Great Flood

There's a great flood happening so the prostitutes and drug dealers have come to seek shelter in the bookstore. Meanwhile as this is all going down it's the last Tuesday night of the month, so we are reading. You can see all the employees running throughout strategically placing buckets on the carpet floor to catch the rain that's coming in through the roof. They respect our time, our sharing. This is a safe place.

There's a gray old lady in a wheelchair with one of her boobs hanging out reading about rain and death, so we don't really care about what's going on outside. Flood you say? That's nice. We are here, that's out there.

Now the rain is really picking up, but even so, we care even less than before. We have other things to be concerned about, like things the lady is talking about in her poem; and for once everyone is listening one-hundred-percent sincerely.

The rain can't be stopped and admittedly most of us are thinking we probably only have a 40% chance of making it out of here alive.

No, you know what, we are going to be fine, that's what someone in the crowd has just said. So, we say okay, and stick around, we believe him, we trust one another.

A second later the roof collapses. We won't be stopped. Someone grabs the lady's wheelchair and we continue out in the parking garage to the top of the roof in order to seek higher ground. We keep reading.

Acknowledgments

Thank you to the editors of the following literary journals where some of these writings were first published:

L' Allure des Mots: 'A Reference to Weather'
Duende: 'It's As If We Never Left'
Pacifica Review: 'Floorboards'
El Portal: 'The History of Furniture and Wood Flooring in East Texas', 'Back in 2003 when watching four TV shows in a row was considered an insane amount of TV watching'
Rollick Magazine: 'For Matthew'
Red Flag Poetry: 'Lucky Them'
Ohio Edit: 'Grand Rapids, Michigan'
Connotation Press: 'acknowledging myself's mistakes', 'before falling out of love', 'a list of things'
Birdy Magazine: 'Dead People Cannibalism'
Maudlin House: 'Birds of America'
Foliate Oak Magazine: 'Mount Pleasant, Michigan'
101 Words: 'Self-Help', 'Things to Do'
Flash Fiction Magazine: 'Local Weather'
Yellow Chair Review: 'When the Cubs Win the World Series'
Severine Lit: 'write talk-talk if you have no one to talk-talk with'
Empty Sink Publishing: 'Somewhere in the Future You Are Remembering Today'

Ginosko Literary Journal: 'Conversations in an Idle Car', 'Filling in'

Platform for Prose: 'Evolution of All Things'

Across the Margin: 'War Time', 'A Brief History of the Great Lakes Region in the 1990s'

The RPD Society: 'Church Poem'

Sick Lit Magazine: 'Drinking Whisky with Leon Trotsky Trout'

Jellyfish Review: 'Deer Michigan'

Firefly Magazine: 'Back to the Beginning'

The Airgonaut: 'home'

Beechwood Review: 'Cities in the Wilderness'

Scrutiny Journal: '49 letters never mailed, to live out their days in a nonexistent shoe-box in a make believe attic'

Bottlecap Press: 'when the water runs out'

Eunoia Review: 'Goodbye Jim Harrison'

CBNGP: 'Drink Pop with Mao'

Thanks

A childhood memory that comes back to me is it's winter, I press my face against the cold window, the snow is coming down, it's evening, and my mother and I are sitting in the living room next to the fireplace. I'm reading my first novel, a Jack London book, and even though I don't know half of the words, you encourage me to keep going. That was a moment, I knew, even then, I would always remember. Thank you.

I would also like to thank my friends for encouraging me to write. Without you none of this would've been written. Near and far, I think of you often.

Thank you Matt Potter for reading my writing and publishing my first book.

Lastly, thank you, dear reader, for taking the time to listen.

About the Author

Jack C. Buck, a Michigan native, now resides in Colorado, where he is a public school teacher. *Deer Michigan* is his first book

Author photograph by Dylan Osborne

Also from Truth Serum Press

http://truthserumpress.net/catalogue/

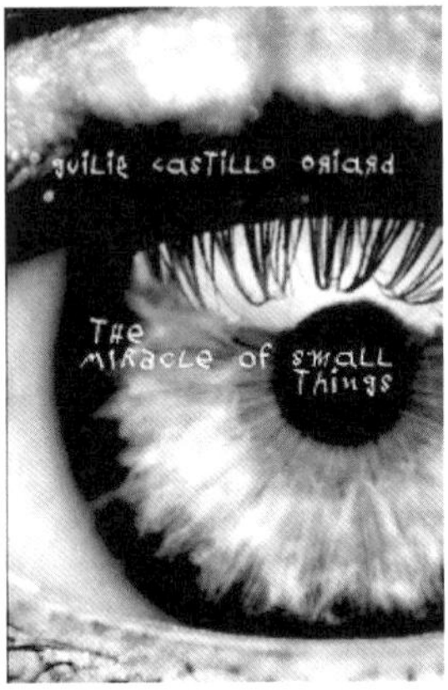

The Miracle of Small Things

by Guilie Castillo Oriard

978-1-925101-73-7 (paperback)
978-1-925101-74-4 (eBook)

The Miracle of Small Things beguiles the reader with a witty and compassionate portrait of a year in the life of Luis Villalobos in tropical Curaçao, where nothing is quite what it seems, and all can be lost or gained in a summer afternoon on the beach. Told deftly, with humor and insight into our very human vulnerabilities, this lovely novella by Guilie Castillo Oriard builds upon that quest for happiness we share, a sense of belonging, and makes me want to travel south to find my own miracle.

Also from Truth Serum Press

http://truthserumpress.net/catalogue/

La Ronde

by Townsend Walker

978-1-925101-64-5 (paperback)
978-1-925101-65-2 (eBook)

Try putting *La Ronde* down after you've begun to read – not possible. It sweeps you up into a beguiling tale of greed, mistaken identity, and desire. Townsend Walker has crafted a chilling novella with characters that pop off the page and events that will make you squirm ... a tale of greed and desire that will make you wonder ... what would your spouse do if he or she wanted to kill you?

Also from Truth Serum Press

http://truthserumpress.net/catalogue/

Based on True Stories

by Matt Potter

978-1-925101-75-1 (paperback)
978-1-925101-76-8 (eBook)

The small fictions in *Based on True Stories* will not lull you – they will piss you off or, at the least, move you to indignation, or tears, or laughter. Maybe all three. These gems provoke, like the tip of a chef's knife pricking skin, and just as the words get uncomfortable, the story delivers the bit of redemption that reveals the humanity of his characters – and of us all. These stories are real, raw, and honest. The reading doesn't get much better than that.

Also from Truth Serum Press

http://truthserumpress.net/catalogue/

Luck and Other Truths

by Richard Mark Glover

978-1-925101-77-5 (paperback)
978-1-925536-04-1 (eBook)

Richard Mark Glover spins larger-than-life tales of folks on the fringe in places where they tend to collect, with the focus on that great empty space known as Far West Texas. What might appear to outsiders as a whole bunch of harsh forbidding nothing – think Cormac McCarthy – these stories are filled with quirky characters brought to life by Glover's observant eye and quirk-spotting pen.

Also from Truth Serum Press

http://truthserumpress.net/catalogue/

Rain Check

by Levi Andrew Noe

978-1-925536-09-6 (paperback)
978-1-925536-10-2 (eBook)

Beautifully rendered, the stories in *Rain Check* could well be the footprints and photographs of our own lives if we'd have taken risks as daring as Noe's characters. Each misstep, triumph and regret rings true. Reading these stories is like being a lucky voyeur who happens upon an artist with brush in hand, nearing the finishing touch of their masterpiece. Nothing is more potent than prose that lifts off the page and lands, like a well-placed bullet or caress, on the heart, and that's precisely what Noe has done here.

Also from Truth Serum Press

http://truthserumpress.net/catalogue/

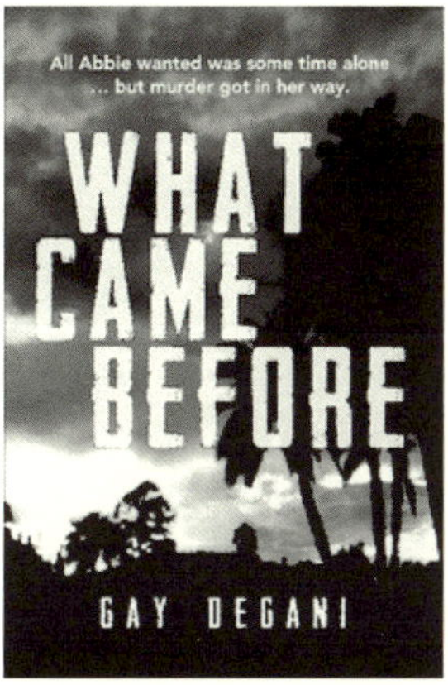

What Came Before

by Gay Degani

978-1-925536-05-8 (paperback)
978-1-925536-06-5 (eBook)

Five words scribbled on a discarded piece of paper ignite old memories for Abbie Palmer, leading to the explosive uncovering of a fifty-year-old mystery. *What Came Before*, Gay Degani's debut novel rumbles along at break-neck speed. I've long enjoyed the quirky characters and tightly-written plots of Ms. Degani's short stories and her novel didn't disappoint me. The book presents great characters, including a strong older-female protagonist and ably-managed twists and turns through the streets and people of modern-day Los Angeles, as well as the L.A. of 50 years ago. Old-school suspense at its best.

Also from Truth Serum Press

http://truthserumpress.net/catalogue/

happyme@t.us

by Kim Conklin

978-1-925536-07-2 (paperback)
978-1-925536-08-9 (eBook)

To be everywhere and nowhere, all at once ... Through her stories, Kim Conklin takes us on a journey of the human condition, where the everyday becomes foreign and dangerous, while the oddities of our world provide us with strange comfort. Each story is unsettling, passionate, thoughtful, provocative and reaffirming; taking the reader everywhere and nowhere, all at once. Dark tales, deftly told.

Also from Truth Serum Press

http://truthserumpress.net/catalogue/

Hello Berlin!

by Jason S. Andrews

978-1-925536-11-9 (paperback)
978-1-925536-12-6 (eBook)

Paul is an average Joe from London. He arrives in Berlin during the exciting noughties and discovers a world of free love, free afternoons and lofty literary pursuits. Clueless and curiously innocent, Paul steals the hearts of those around him, leading to anything but a tender love story. Fresh and honest.